The Kitten Psychologist Tries To Be Patient Through Email

THEA VAN DIEPEN

OTHER WORKS

WHITE CHANGELING SERIES

Hidden In Sealskin
Like Mist Over The Eyes

THE UNDEAD FAIRY TALES COLLECTION

The Illuminated Heart

Dreaming Of Her And Other Stories
The Tree Remembers

Find other works by the author at
https://www.theavandiepen.com

The Kitten Psychologist Tries

To Be Patient Through

Email

INKLETS #12

THEA VAN DIEPEN

AMY LAURENS

Inkprint
PRESS

www.inkprintpress.com

This is a work of fiction. All characters,
organisations and events are the author's creation,
or are used fictitiously.

ISBN: 978-1-925825-11-4
eBook ISBN: 9781386782551

www.inkprintpress.com

*National Library of Australia Cataloguing-in-Publication
Data*
van Diepen, Thea
The Kitten Psychologist Tries To Be Patient
Through Email
28 p.
ISBN: 978-1-925825-11-4
Inkprint Press, Canberra, Australia
1. Fiction—Animals 2. Fiction—Short Stories

First Print Edition: June 2019
Cover design © Inkprint Press
Interior art © Amy Laurens

THE KITTEN PSYCHOLOGIST TRIES TO BE PATIENT THROUGH EMAIL

Dear Kitten,

I would absolutely love to speak with you, but your humans, as you say, have decided I can't ever see you. You'll have to deal with the Tumblr thing on your own.

Sincerely,
Your psychologist

Dear psychologist human,

There is no reason to be rude with me. As you see perfectly well, we can talk through email. Your payment will be minimal to none as a result, but I still need your help, so you are still my psychologist.

My current dilemma has less to do with Tumblr and more to do with the conversation you had with my humans. I overheard you, you know. What is this nonsense about cats not being moral? We are most certainly moral. Explain this to me.

I also seem to be having difficulties accessing my humans' bank account. Do you have any solutions to that?

Sincerely,
You know who

Dear kitten,

That's… not really how being a psychologist works. It's a job. I need to get paid.

And, while I disagree with your owners on principle, your last paragraph sort of proves their point.

Sincerely,
Your psychologist

Dear psychologist human,

Thank you for Skyping with me again. Finally. I hope you now understand the unfeasibility of my obtaining employment (not to mention a bank account of my own) in order to pay you. This really isn't a moral matter so much as a pragmatic one.

I am a kitten. And I live in a world where kittens cannot get jobs. I, therefore, cannot get paid. You will have to help me, regardless.

Meanwhile, I've noticed my humans are more attentive to me of late. Not in the way I like. They have been keeping me from doing as I please in regards to electronics and leaving the house.

Speaking to them about the matter has changed nothing.

How do I convince them that I am perfectly capable and trustworthy enough to be left on my own?

Sincerely,
You know who

Dear kitten,

If you're actually going to take any advice I give, you're going to pay me. Or work something else out. Otherwise, you're telling me that you're not trustworthy and that working for you isn't working for you. It's you using me.

Which, while I'm being perfectly honest with you, is what you've been doing with your owners.

Sincerely,
Your psychologist

Dammit. Maybe I shouldn't have worded that so strongly, but I'd sent it before I could stop myself. I'd been emailing my friends, too. They wanted to know how to deal with their kitten, and I'd agreed to give them free sessions in exchange for keeping the money the kitten had paid me from their bank account.

It was one of those things you know is a bad idea, but you're too worried about what might happen if you don't that you say yes to it anyways.

Those sessions were... hard. They're my friends, but I had to be their psychologist instead and, let me tell you, telling your friends to solve their own problems doesn't ever go over very well. Especially when they're dead set against it. All they wanted to do was figure out what to do to get the kitten to do what they wanted. All I wanted was to get them out of my office before I yelled at them.

I freak out over my finances too much. If I hadn't, I never would have been in this situation. Now, if I could just get a time machine and go tell my past self that, that would be great.

Oh. A new email. Great.

Dear psychologist human,

And how, exactly, do you propose I "work something else out"?

Sincerely,
You know who

I could always turn off my computer and pretend I hadn't read that. Or that my email had glitched and I'd never received the message.

Except that I'm doing that thing where I'm trying to get out of this darn mess.

Dear kitten,

Talk to your owners about it. And don't let them tell you you're not able to do anything. The moment you're feeling helpless or powerless or incapable is the moment you've started going in the wrong direction.

Sincerely,
Your psychologist

Dear psychologist human,

I am never helpless, powerless, or incapable. I am a feline. But I will speak to them, since you obviously didn't know what you meant in the first place.

Sincerely,
You know who

I'm never going to get over getting emails from a kitten that's basically telling me it's Voldemort. It's certainly mean enough to be him.

I wrote an angry reply which I deleted right afterwards as I sat back in my chair and sighed.

Seven or so additional deleted angry replies later, another email arrived in my inbox. Two emails, actually.

Dear psychologist human,

You have a devious mind. I like you.

Sincerely,
You know who

And then, from my friends:

You're not going to believe what our kitten just did. Can we have our next session earlier in the week?

I'm not sure what to feel about this.
...
I'm really not sure what to feel about this.

To my friends:

I'm open on Wednesday between 3pm and 5pm. Does that work for you?

It's amazing what you can do on autopilot.

From my friends:

Yes, 3pm. This can't wait.

Uh oh. What did the kitten go and do now?
And how am I going to get out of this with my skin intact?

THE MAKING OF
THE KITTEN PSYCHOLOGIST TRIES TO BE PATIENT THROUGH EMAIL

While epistolary novels have yet to make it to my bibliography, I figured it would be *hilarious* to write this as a series of emails between the psychologist and kitten. After all, *The Kitten Psychologist vs the Kitten's Owners* had ended with an email. And, well, I figured readers would have read enough to be able to fill in the blanks. Like an inside joke. In the middle of a series. Which had basically been a series of therapy sessions for me.

Oh boy.

I had also hoped that this series would be brought to an end, say, a story ago, and it became increasingly clear as I wrote this one that I had at least one more instalment to go. But how would it end? I was already trying to write to an ending I knew nothing about, since I hadn't planned this series *at all* aside from "Ha ha, wouldn't it be fun to write about a kitten with a psychologist?" and since I was simultaneously working through my own life problems through the writing of these stories.

You can't really plan endings when you're being your own psychologist. You either get there, or you stop.

So I sat down, wrote to the end, and hoped like heck that I would find the end soon.

DOWNLOAD YOUR FREE EBOOK

When you buy a print book from Inkprint Press, we like to say THANK YOU by offering you the ebook for free!

Please head to www.inkprintpress.com/inklets/12/ and the use the coupon INK12 to get your copy of this Inklet in epub AND mobi today!
(Coupon will only work once.)

DREAMING OF HER
AND OTHER
STORIES

A collection of short stories and poetry, written as refreshers, reminders of what makes life beautiful. Pieces include a story of the life of a river as he discovers his true self, a poetic retelling of Daphne's flight from Apollo, and, in the titular story, a literal nightmare as a girl comes to terms with the death of her sister.

https://www.theavandiepen.com

ABOUT THE AUTHOR

THEA VAN DIEPEN spent the first ten years of her life on a tree-wrapped acreage where an inquisitive child might believe in magic. Nowadays, she lives in Edmonton, breathing life into stories in the form of books such as the *White Changeling* series, a webcomic, and a video game.

Her website is theavandiepen.com, where she can be contacted in English and French... so long as you don't ask her to count in French, as she tends to miss numbers ending in six entirely by accident.

INKLETS

Collect them all! Released on the 1st and 15th of each month.

SEVENTY
LIANA BROOKS

A Final Request
for Mercy
AMY LAURENS

the kitten psychologist
vs.
the kitten's owners
THEA VAN DIEPEN

Answer the
Question
AMY LAURENS

Happily,
Red
AMY LAURENS

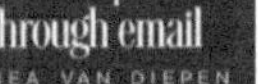

the kitten psychologist
tries to be patient
through email
THEA VAN DIEPEN

DRAGON
Tuesday
AMY LAURENS

RED PLANET
REFUGEES
LIANA BROOKS

the kitten psychologist &
What The Kitten Did
THEA VAN DIEPEN

INKLET #016
Cherry Blossom
AMY LAURENS

INKLET #017
Alone
AMY LAURENS

INKLET #018
the kitten psychologist
& The Kitten
Come To A Conclusion
THEA VAN DIEPEN

INKLET #019
LEVEL NINE
LIANA BROOKS

INKLET #020
To Dust
AMY LAURENS

INKLET #021
Interchange
AMY LAURENS

INKLET #022
Emalia's Lanterns
LIANA BROOKS

INKLET #023
Dear Santa
AMY LAURENS

INKLET #024
The Quilt-Maker's Scrap
AMY LAURENS